Mrs Ball...

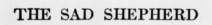

THE SAD SHEPHERD

THE
SAD SHEPHERD

A CHRISTMAS STORY

BY

HENRY VAN DYKE

NEW YORK
CHARLES SCRIBNER'S SONS
1911

THE SAD SHEPHERD

THE SAD SHEPHERD

I

DARKNESS

OUT of the Valley of Gardens, where a film of new-fallen snow lay smooth as feathers on the breast of a dove, the ancient Pools of Solomon looked up into the night sky with dark, tranquil eyes, wide-open and passive, reflecting the crisp stars and the small, round moon. The full springs, overflowing on the hill-side, melted their way through the field of white in winding channels; and along their course the grass was green even in the dead of winter.

[3]

But the sad shepherd walked far above the friendly valley, in a region where ridges of gray rock welted and scarred the back of the earth, like wounds of half-forgotten strife and battles long ago. The solitude was forbidding and disquieting; the keen air that searched the wanderer had no pity in it; and the myriad glances of the night were curiously cold.

His flock straggled after him. The sheep, weather-beaten and dejected, followed the path with low heads nodding from side to side, as if they had travelled far and found little pasture. The black, lop-eared goats leaped upon the rocks, restless and ravenous, tearing down the tender branches and leaves of the dwarf oaks and wild olives. They reared up against the twisted trunks and

[4]

crawled and scrambled among the boughs. It was like a company of gray downcast friends and a troop of merry little black devils following the sad shepherd afar off.

He walked looking on the ground, paying small heed to them. Now and again, when the sound of pattering feet and panting breath and the rustling and rending among the copses fell too far behind, he drew out his shepherd's pipe and blew a strain of music, shrill and plaintive, quavering and lamenting through the hollow night. He waited while the troops of gray and black scuffled and bounded and trotted near to him. Then he dropped the pipe into its place again and strode forward, looking on the ground.

The fitful, shivery wind that rasped

the hill-top, fluttered the rags of his long mantle of Tyrian blue, torn by thorns and stained by travel. The rich tunic of striped silk beneath it was worn thin, and the girdle about his loins had lost all its ornaments of silver and jewels. His curling hair hung down dishevelled under a turban of fine linen, in which the gilt threads were frayed and tarnished; and his shoes of soft leather were broken by the road. On his brown fingers the places of the vanished rings were still marked in white skin. He carried not the long staff nor the heavy nail-studded rod of the shepherd, but a slender stick of carved cedar battered and scratched by hard usage, and the handle, which must once have been of precious metal, was missing.

He was a strange figure for that lonely place and that humble occupation—a branch of faded beauty from some royal garden tossed by rude winds into the wilderness—a pleasure craft adrift, buffeted and broken, on rough seas.

But he seemed to have passed beyond caring. His young face was frayed and threadbare as his garments. The splendor of the moonlight flooding the wild world meant as little to him as the hardness of the rugged track which he followed. He wrapped his tattered mantle closer around him, and strode ahead, looking on the ground.

As the path dropped from the summit of the ridge toward the Valley of Mills and passed among huge broken rocks, three men sprang at

[7]

him from the shadows. He lifted his
stick, but let it fall again, and a
strange ghost of a smile twisted his
face as they gripped him and threw
him down.

"You are rough beggars," he said.
"Say what you want, you are welcome to it."

"Your money, dog of a courtier,"
they muttered fiercely; "give us your
golden collar, Herod's hound, quick,
or you die!"

"The quicker the better," he answered, closing his eyes.

The bewildered flock of sheep and
goats, gathered in a silent ring, stood
at gaze while the robbers fumbled
over their master

"This is a stray dog," said one, "he
has lost his collar, there is not even
the price of a mouthful of wine on

him. Shall we kill him and leave him
for the vultures?"

"What have the vultures done for
us," said another, "that we should
feed them? Let us take his cloak and
drive off his flock, and leave him to
die in his own time."

With a kick and a curse they left
him. He opened his eyes and lay
quiet for a moment, with his twisted
smile, watching the stars.

"You creep like snails," he said. "I
thought you had marked my time to-
night. But not even that is given to
me for nothing. I must pay for all, it
seems."

Far away, slowly scattering and re-
ceding, he heard the rustling and
bleating of his frightened flock as the
robbers, running and shouting, tried
to drive them over the hills. Then he

stood up and took the shepherd's
pipe, a worthless bit of reed, from the
breast of his tunic. He blew again
that plaintive, piercing air, sounding
it out over the ridges and distant
thickets. It seemed to have neither
beginning nor end; a melancholy,
pleading tune that searched forever
after something lost.

While he played, the sheep and the
goats, slipping away from their cap-
tors by roundabout ways, hiding
behind the laurel bushes, following
the dark gullies, leaping down the
broken cliffs, came circling back to
him, one after another; and as they
came, he interrupted his playing,
now and then, to call them by name.

When they were nearly all assem-
bled, he went down swiftly toward
the lower valley, and they followed

him, panting. At the last crook of the path on the steep hillside a straggler came after him along the cliff. He looked up and saw it outlined against the sky. Then he saw it leap, and slip, and fall beyond the path into a deep cleft.

"Little fool," he said, "fortune is kind to you! You have escaped from the big trap of life. What? You are crying for help? You are still in the trap? Then I must go down to you, little fool, for I am a fool too. But why I must do it, I know no more than you know."

He lowered himself quickly and perilously into the cleft, and found the creature with its leg broken and bleeding. It was not a sheep but a young goat. He had no cloak to wrap it in, but he took off his turban and unrolled it, and bound it around the trembling animal. Then he climbed back to the path and strode on at the head of his flock, carrying the little black kid in his arms.

There were houses in the Valley of the Mills; and in some of them lights were burning; and the drone of the mill-stones, where the women were still grinding, came out into the night like the humming of drowsy bees. As the women heard the pattering and bleating of the flock, they wondered who was passing so late. One of them, in a house where there was no mill but many lights, came to the door and looked out laughing, her face and bosom bare.

But the sad shepherd did not stay. His long shadow and the confused mass of lesser shadows behind him

[12]

drifted down the white moonlight, past the yellow bars of lamplight that gleamed from the doorways. It seemed as if he were bound to go somewhere and would not delay.

Yet with all his haste to be gone, it was plain that he thought little of where he was going. For when he came to the foot of the valley, where the paths divided, he stood between them staring vacantly, without a desire to turn him this way or that. The imperative of choice halted him like a barrier. The balance of his mind hung even because both scales were empty. He could act, he could go, for his strength was untouched; but he could not choose, for his will was broken within him.

The path to the left went up toward the little town of Bethlehem, with huddled roofs and walls in silhouette along the double-crested hill. It was dark and forbidding as a closed fortress. The sad shepherd looked at it with indifferent eyes; there was nothing there to draw him.

The path to the right wound through rock-strewn valleys toward the Dead Sea. But rising out of that crumpled wilderness, a mile or two away, the smooth white ribbon of a chariot-road lay upon the flank of a cone-shaped mountain and curled in loops toward its peak. There the great cone was cut squarely off, and the levelled summit was capped by a palace of marble, with round towers at the corners and flaring beacons along the walls; and the glow of an immense fire, hidden in the central court-yard, painted a false dawn in the eastern sky. All

[14]

down the clean-cut mountain slopes, on terraces and blind arcades, the lights flashed from lesser pavilions and pleasure-houses.

It was the secret orchard of Herod and his friends, their trysting-place with the spirits of mirth and madness. They called it the Mountain of the Little Paradise. Rich gardens were there; and the cool water from the Pools of Solomon plashed in the fountains; and trees of the knowledge of good and evil fruited blood-red and ivory-white above them; and smooth, curving, glistening shapes, whispering softly of pleasure, lay among the flowers and glided behind the trees. All this was now hidden in the dark. Only the strange bulk of the mountain, a sharp black pyramid girdled and crowned with fire, loomed across

[15]

the night—a mountain once seen never to be forgotten.

The sad shepherd remembered it well. He looked at it with the eyes of a child who has been in hell. It burned him from afar. Turning neither to the right nor to the left, he walked without a path straight out upon the plain of Bethlehem, still whitened in the hollows and on the sheltered side of its rounded hillocks by the veil of snow.

He faced a wide and empty world. To the west in sleeping Bethlehem, to the east in flaring Herodium, the life of man was infinitely far away from him. Even the stars seemed to withdraw themselves against the blue-black of the sky. They diminished and receded till they were like pin-holes in the vault above him. The

[16]

moon in mid-heaven shrank into a bit of burnished silver, hard and glittering, immeasurably remote. The ragged, inhospitable ridges of Tekoa lay stretched in mortal slumber along the horizon, and between them he caught a glimpse of the sunken Lake of Death, darkly gleaming in its deep bed. There was no movement, no sound, on the plain where he walked, except the soft-padding feet of his dumb, obsequious flock.

He felt an endless isolation strike cold to his heart, against which he held the limp body of the wounded kid, wondering the while, with a half-contempt for his own foolishness, why he took such trouble to save a tiny scrap of the worthless tissue which is called life.

Even when a man does not know or

care where he is going, if he steps on-
ward he will get there. In an hour or
more of walking over the plain the sad
shepherd came to a sheep-fold of gray
stones with a rude tower beside it.
The fold was full of sheep, and at the
foot of the tower a little fire of thorns
was burning, around which four
shepherds were crouching, wrapped
in their thick woollen cloaks.

As the stranger approached they
looked up, and one of them rose
quickly to his feet, grasping his
knotted club. But when they saw the
flock that followed the sad shepherd,
they stared at each other and said:
"It is one of us, a keeper of sheep.
But how comes he here in this rai-
ment? It is what men wear in kings'
houses."

"No," said the one who was standing, "it is what they wear when they have been thrown out of them. Look at the rags. He may be a thief and a robber with his stolen flock."

"Salute him when he comes near," said the oldest shepherd. "Are we not four to one? We have nothing to fear from a ragged traveller. Speak him fair. It is the will of God—and it costs nothing."

"Peace be with you, brother," cried the youngest shepherd; "may your mother and father be blessed."

"May your heart be enlarged," the stranger answered, "and may all your families be more blessed than mine, for I have none."

"A homeless man," said the old shepherd, "has either been robbed by his fellows, or punished by God."

[19]

"I do not know which it was," answered the stranger; "the end is the same, as you see."

"By your speech you come from Galilee. Where are you going? What are you seeking here?"

"I was going nowhere, my masters; but it was cold on the way there, and my feet turned to your fire."

"Come then, if you are a peaceable man, and warm your feet with us. Heat is a good gift; divide it and it is not less. But you shall have bread and salt too, if you will."

"May your hospitality enrich you. I am your unworthy guest. But my flock?"

"Let your flock shelter by the south wall of the fold: there is good picking there and no wind. Come you and sit with us."

So they all sat down by the fire; and the sad shepherd ate of their bread, but sparingly, like a man to whom hunger brings a need but no joy in the satisfying of it; and the others were silent for a proper time, out of courtesy. Then the oldest shepherd spoke:

"My name is Zadok the son of Eliezer, of Bethlehem. I am the chief shepherd of the flocks of the Temple, which are before you in the fold. These are my sister's sons, Jotham, and Shama, and Nathan: their father Elkanah is dead; and but for these I am a childless man."

"My name," replied the stranger, "is Ammiel the son of Jochanan, of the city of Bethsaida, by the Sea of Galilee, and I am a fatherless man."

"It is better to be childless than fatherless," said Zadok, "yet it is the

will of God that children should bury
their fathers. When did the blessed
Jochanan die?"

"I know not whether he be dead or
alive. It is three years since I looked
upon his face or had word of him."

"You are an exile then? he has cast
you off?"

"It was the other way," said Ammiel, looking on the ground.

At this the shepherd Shama, who
had listened with doubt in his face,
started up in anger. "Pig of a Gali-
lean," he cried, "despiser of parents!
breaker of the law! When I saw you
coming I knew you for something
vile. Why do you darken the night for
us with your presence? You have re-
viled him who begot you. Away, or
we stone you!"

Ammiel did not answer or move.

The twisted smile passed over his
bowed face again as he waited to
know the shepherds' will with him,
even as he had waited for the robbers.
But Zadok lifted his hand.

"Not so hasty, Shama-ben-Elkanah.
You also break the law by judging a
man unheard. The rabbis have told
us that there is a tradition of the elders—a rule as holy as the law itself—
that a man may deny his father in a
certain way without sin. It is a strange
rule, and it must be very holy or it
would not be so strange. But this is
the teaching of the elders: a son may
say of anything for which his father
asks him—a sheep, or a measure of
corn, or a field, or a purse of silver—
'it is Corban, a gift that I have vowed
unto the Lord;' and so his father shall
have no more claim upon him. Have

you said 'Corban' to your father,
Ammiel-ben-Jochanan? Have you
made a vow unto the Lord?"

"I have said 'Corban,'" answered
Ammiel, lifting his face, still shad-
owed by that strange smile, "but it
was not the Lord who heard my
vow."

"Tell us what you have done," said
the old man sternly, "for we will
neither judge you, nor shelter you,
unless we hear your story."

"There is nothing in it," replied
Ammiel indifferently. "It is an old
story. But if you are curious you shall
hear it. Afterward you shall deal with
me as you will."

So the shepherds, wrapped in their
warm cloaks, sat listening with grave
faces and watchful, unsearchable
eyes, while Ammiel in his tattered

silk sat by the sinking fire of thorns
and told his tale with a voice that had
no room for hope or fear—a cool,
dead voice that spoke only of things
ended.

II

"IN my father's house I was the second son. My brother was honored and trusted in all things. He was a prudent man and profitable to the household. All that he counselled was done, all that he wished he had. My place was a narrow one. There was neither honor nor joy in it, for it was filled with daily tasks and rebukes. No one cared for me. My mother sometimes wept when I was rebuked. Perhaps she was disappointed in me. But she had no power to make things better. I felt that I was a beast of burden, fed only in order that I might be useful; and the dull life irked me like an ill-fitting harness. There was nothing in it.

"I went to my father and claimed my share of the inheritance. He was rich. He gave it to me. It did not impoverish him and it made me free. I said to him 'Corban,' and shook the dust of Bethsaida from my feet.

"I went out to look for mirth and love and joy and all that is pleasant to the eyes and sweet to the taste. If a god made me, thought I, he made me to live, and the pride of life was strong in my heart and in my flesh. My vow was offered to that well-known god. I served him in Jerusalem, in Alexandria, in Rome, for his altars are everywhere and men worship him openly or in secret.

"My money and youth made me welcome to his followers, and I spent them both freely as if they could never come to an end. I clothed myself in purple and fine linen and fared sumptuously every day. The wine of Cyprus and the dishes of Egypt and Syria were on my table. My dwelling was crowded with merry guests. They came for what I gave them. Their faces were hungry and their soft touch was like the clinging of leeches. To them I was nothing but money and youth; no longer a beast of burden—a beast of pleasure. There was nothing in it.

"From the richest fare my heart went away empty, and after the wildest banquet my soul fell drunk and solitary into sleep.

"Then I thought, Power is better than pleasure. If a man will feast and revel let him do it with the great. They will favor him, and raise him up for the service that he renders them. He will obtain place and authority in the world and gain many friends. So I joined myself to Herod."

When the sad shepherd spoke this name his listeners drew back from him as if it were a defilement to hear it. They spat upon the ground and cursed the Idumean who called himself their king.

"A slave!" Jotham cried, "a bloody tyrant and a slave from Edom! A fox, a vile beast who devours his own children! God burn him in Gehenna."

The old Zadok picked up a stone and threw it into the darkness, saying slowly, "I cast this stone on the grave of the Idumean, the blasphemer, the defiler of the Temple! God send us soon the Deliverer, the Promised One, the true King of Israel!" Ammiel made no sign, but went on with his story.

"Herod used me well,—for his own purpose. He welcomed me to his palace and his table, and gave me a place among his favorites. He was so much my friend that he borrowed my money. There were many of the nobles of Jerusalem with him, Sadducees, and proselytes from Rome and Asia, and women from everywhere. The law of Israel was observed in the open court, when the people were watching. But in the secret feasts there was no law but the will of Herod, and many deities were served but no god was worshipped. There the captains and the princes of Rome consorted with the high-priest and his sons by night; and there was much coming and going by hidden ways. Everybody was a borrower or a lender, a buyer or a seller of favors. It was a house of diligent madness. There was nothing in it.

"In the midst of this whirling life a great need of love came upon me and I wished to hold some one in my inmost heart.

"At a certain place in the city, within closed doors, I saw a young slave-girl dancing. She was about fifteen years old, thin and supple; she danced like a reed in the wind; but her eyes were weary as death, and her white body was marked with bruises. She stumbled, and the men laughed at her. She fell, and her mistress beat her, crying out that she would fain be rid of such a heavy-footed slave. I paid the price and took her to my dwelling.

"Her name was Tamar. She was a daughter of Lebanon. I robed her in silk and broidered linen. I nourished her with tender care so that beauty came upon her like the blossoming of an almond tree; she was a garden enclosed, breathing spices. Her eyes were like doves behind her veil, her lips were a thread of scarlet, her neck was a tower of ivory, and her breasts were as two fawns which feed among the lilies. She was whiter than milk, and more rosy than the flower of the peach, and her dancing was like the flight of a bird among the branches. So I loved her.

"She lay in my bosom as a clear stone that one has bought and polished and set in fine gold at the end

of a golden chain. Never was she glad
at my coming or sorry at my going.
Never did she give me anything except what I took from her. There was
nothing in it.

"Now whether Herod knew of the
jewel that I kept in my dwelling I
cannot tell. It was sure that he had
his spies in all the city, and himself
walked the streets by night in a dis-
guise. On a certain day he sent for
me, and had me into his secret
chamber, professing great love toward me and more confidence than in
any man that lived. So I must go
to Rome for him, bearing a sealed
letter and a private message to
Cæsar. All my goods would be left
safely in the hands of the king, my
friend, who would reward me double.
There was a certain place of high

authority at Jerusalem which Cæsar would gladly bestow on a Jew who had done him a service. This mission would commend me to him. It was a great occasion, suited to my powers. Thus Herod fed me with fair promises, and I ran his errand. There was nothing in it.

"I stood before Cæsar and gave him the letter. He read it and laughed, saying that a prince with an incurable hunger is a servant of value to an emperor. Then he asked me if there was nothing sent with the letter. I answered that there was no gift, but a message for his private ear. He drew me aside and I told him that Herod begged earnestly that his dear son, Antipater, might be sent back in haste from Rome to Palestine, for the king had great need of him.

"At this Cæsar laughed again. 'To bury him, I suppose,' said he, 'with his brothers, Alexander and Aristobulus! Truly, it is better to be Herod's swine than his son. Tell the old fox he may catch his own prey.' With this he turned from me and I withdrew unrewarded, to make my way back, as best I could with an empty purse, to Palestine. I had seen the Lord of the World. There was nothing in it.

"Selling my rings and bracelets I got passage in a trading ship for Joppa. There I heard that the king was not in Jerusalem, at his Palace of the Upper City, but had gone with his friends to make merry for a month on the Mountain of the Little Paradise. On that hill-top over against us, where the lights are flaring to-night,

in the banquet-hall where couches
are spread for a hundred guests, I
found Herod."

The listening shepherds spat upon
the ground again, and Jotham muttered, "May the worms that devour
his flesh never die!" But Zadok
whispered, "We wait for the Lord's
salvation to come out of Zion." And
the sad shepherd, looking with fixed
eyes at the firelit mountain far away,
continued his story:

"The king lay on his ivory couch,
and the sweat of his disease was heavy
upon him, for he was old, and his
flesh was corrupted. But his hair and
his beard were dyed and perfumed
and there was a wreath of roses on
his head. The hall was full of nobles
and great men, the sons of the high-
priest were there, and the servants

poured their wine in cups of gold. There was a sound of soft music; and all the men were watching a girl who danced in the middle of the hall; and the eyes of Herod were fiery, like the eyes of a fox.

"The dancer was Tamar. She glistened like the snow on Lebanon, and the redness of her was ruddier than a pomegranate, and her dancing was like the coiling of white serpents. When the dance was ended her attendants threw a veil of gauze over her and she lay among her cushions, half covered with flowers, at the feet of the king.

"Through the sound of clapping hands and shouting, two slaves led me behind the couch of Herod. His eyes narrowed as they fell upon me. I told him the message of Cæsar, making it soft, as if it were a word that suffered him to catch his prey. He stroked his beard softly and his look fell on Tamar. 'I have caught it,' he murmured; 'by all the gods, I have always caught it. And my dear son, Antipater, is coming home of his own will. I have lured him, he is mine.'

"Then a look of madness crossed his face and he sprang up, with frothing lips, and struck at me. 'What is this,' he cried, 'a spy, a servant of my false son, a traitor in my banquet-hall! Who are you?' I knelt before him, protesting that he must know me; that I was his friend, his messenger; that I had left all my goods in his hands; that the girl who had danced for him was mine. At this his face changed again and he fell back on his couch, shaken with hor-

[38]

rible laughter. 'Yours!' he cried,
'when was she yours? What is yours?
I know you now, poor madman. You
are Ammiel, a crazy shepherd from
Galilee, who troubled us some time
since. Take him away, slaves. He has
twenty sheep and twenty goats among
my flocks at the foot of the mountain.
See to it that he gets them, and drive
him away.'

"I fought against the slaves with
my bare hands, but they held me. I
called to Tamar, begging her to have
pity on me, to speak for me, to come
with me. She looked up with her eyes
like doves behind her veil, but there
was no knowledge of me in them.
She laughed lazily, as if it were a poor
comedy, and flung a broken rose-
branch in my face. Then the silver
cord was loosened within me, and my

heart went out, and I struggled no more. There was nothing in it.

"Afterward I found myself on the road with this flock. I led them past Hebron into the south country, and so by the Vale of Eshcol, and over many hills beyond the Pools of Solomon, until my feet brought me to your fire. Here I rest on the way to nowhere."

He sat silent, and the four shepherds looked at him with amazement.

"It is a bitter tale," said Shama, "and you are a great sinner."

"I should be a fool not to know that," answered the sad shepherd, "but the knowledge does me no good."

"You must repent," said Nathan, the youngest shepherd, in a friendly voice.

"How can a man repent," answered the sad shepherd, "unless he has hope? But I am sorry for everything, and most of all for living."

"Would you not live to kill the fox Herod?" cried Jotham fiercely.

"Why should I let him out of the trap," answered the sad shepherd. "Is he not dying more slowly than I could kill him?"

"You must have faith in God," said Zadok earnestly and gravely.

"He is too far away."

"Then you must have love for your neighbor."

"He is too near. My confidence in man was like a pool by the wayside. It was shallow, but there was water in it, and sometimes a star shone there. Now the feet of many beasts have trampled through it, and the jackals have drunken of it, and there is no more water. It is dry and the mire is caked at the bottom. '

"Is there nothing good in the world?"

"There is pleasure, but I am sick of it. There is power, but I hate it. There is wisdom, but I mistrust it. Life is a game and every player is for his own hand. Mine is played. I have nothing to win or lose."

"You are young, you have many years to live."

"I am old, yet the days before me are too many."

"But you travel the road, you go forward. Do you hope for nothing?"

"I hope for nothing," said the sad shepherd. "Yet if one thing should come to me it might be the beginning of hope. If I saw in man or woman a

[42]

deed of kindness without a selfish reason, and a proof of love gladly given for its own sake only, then might I turn my face toward that light. Till that comes, how can I have faith in God whom I have never seen? I have seen the world which he has made, and it brings me no faith. There is nothing in it."

"Ammiel-ben-Jochanan," said the old man sternly, "you are a son of Israel, and we have had compassion on you, according to the law. But you are an apostate, an unbeliever, and we can have no more fellowship with you, lest a curse come upon us. The company of the desperate brings misfortune. Go your way and depart from us, for our way is not yours."

So the sad shepherd thanked them for their entertainment, and took the little kid again in his arms, and went into the night, calling his flock. But the youngest shepherd Nathan followed him a few steps and said:

"There is a broken fold at the foot of the hill. It is old and small, but you may find a shelter there for your flock where the wind will not shake you. Go your way with God, brother, and see better days."

Then Ammiel went a little way down the hill and sheltered his flock in a corner of the crumbling walls. He lay among the sheep and the goats with his face upon his folded arms, and whether the time passed slowly or swiftly he did not know, for he slept.

He waked as Nathan came running and stumbling among the scattered stones.

"We have seen a vision," he cried,

"a wonderful vision of angels. Did you not hear them? They sang loudly of the Hope of Israel. We are going to Bethlehem to see this thing which is come to pass. Come you and keep watch over our sheep while we are gone."

"Of angels I have seen and heard nothing," said Ammiel, "but I will guard your flocks with mine, since I am in debt to you for bread and fire."

So he brought the kid in his arms, and the weary flock straggling after him, to the south wall of the great fold again, and sat there by the embers at the foot of the tower, while the others were away.

The moon rested like a ball on the edge of the western hills and rolled behind them. The stars faded in the east and the fires went out on the

Mountain of the Little Paradise.
Over the hills of Moab a gray flood
of dawn rose slowly, and arrows of
red shot far up before the sunrise.

The shepherds returned full of joy
and told what they had seen.

"It was even as the angels said unto
us," said Shama, "and it must be
true. The King of Israel has come.
The faithful shall be blessed."

"Herod shall fall," cried Jotham,
lifting his clenched fist toward the
dark peaked mountain. "Burn, black
Idumean, in the bottomless pit, where
the fire is not quenched."

Zadok spoke more quietly. "We
found the new-born child of whom
the angels told us wrapped in swad-
dling clothes and lying in a manger.
The ways of God are wonderful. His
salvation comes out of darkness, and

[46]

we trust in the promised deliverance. But you, Ammiel-ben-Jochanan, except you believe, you shall not see it. Yet since you have kept our flocks faithfully, and because of the joy that has come to us, I give you this piece of silver to help you on your way."

But Nathan came close to the sad shepherd and touched him on the shoulder with a friendly hand. "Go you also to Bethlehem," he said in a low voice, "for it is good to see what we have seen, and we will keep your flock until you return."

"I will go," said Ammiel, looking into his face, "for I think you wish me well. But whether I shall see what you have seen, or whether I shall ever return, I know not. Farewell."

III

THE narrow streets of Bethlehem were waking to the first stir of life as the sad shepherd came into the town with the morning, and passed through them like one walking in his sleep.

The court-yard of the great khan and the open rooms around it were crowded with travellers, rousing from their night's rest and making ready for the day's journey. In front of the stables half hollowed in the rock beside the inn, men were saddling their horses and their beasts of burden, and there was much noise and confusion.

But beyond these, at the end of the line, there was a deeper grotto in the rock, which was used only when the nearer stalls were full. At the entrance of this an ass was tethered, and a man of middle age stood in the doorway.

The sad shepherd saluted him and told his name.

"I am Joseph the carpenter of Nazareth," replied the man. "Have you also seen the angels of whom your brother shepherds came to tell us?"

"I have seen no angels," answered Ammiel, "nor have I any brothers among the shepherds. But I would fain see what they have seen."

"It is our first-born son," said Joseph, "and the Most High has sent him to us. He is a marvellous child:

[49]

great things are foretold of him.
You may go in, but quietly, for
the child and his mother Mary are
asleep."

So the sad shepherd went in quietly.
His long shadow entered before him,
for the sunrise was flowing into the
door of the grotto. It was made
clean and put in order, and a bed
of straw was laid in the corner on the
ground.

The child was asleep, but the young
mother was waking, for she had
taken him from the manger into her
lap, where her maiden veil of white
was spread to receive him. And she
was singing very softly as she bent
over him in wonder and content.

Ammiel saluted her and kneeled
down to look at the child. He saw
nothing different from other young

children. The mother waited for him
to speak of angels, as the other shepherds had done. The sad shepherd
did not speak, but only looked. And
as he looked his face changed.

"You have suffered pain and dan-
ger and sorrow for his sake," he said
gently.

"They are past," she answered,
"and for his sake I have suffered
them gladly."

"He is very little and helpless; you
must bear many troubles for his
sake."

"To care for him is my joy, and to
bear him lightens my burden."

"He does not know you, he can do
nothing for you."

"But I know him. I have carried
him under my heart, he is my son and
my king."

"Why do you love him?"

The mother looked up at the sad shepherd with a great reproach in her soft eyes. Then her look grew pitiful as it rested on his face.

"You are a sorrowful man," she said.

"I am a wicked man," he answered.

She shook her head gently.

"I know nothing of that," she said, "but you must be very sorrowful, since you are born of a woman and yet you ask a mother why she loves her child. I love him for love's sake, because God has given him to me."

So the mother Mary leaned over her little son again and began to croon a song as if she were alone with him.

But Ammiel was still there, watching and thinking and beginning to re-

member. It came back to him that
there was a woman in Galilee who
had wept when he was rebuked; whose
eyes had followed him when he was
unhappy, as if she longed to do something for him; whose voice had
broken and dropped silent while she
covered her tear-stained face when
he went away.

His thoughts flowed swiftly and
silently toward her and after her like
rapid waves of light. There was a
thought of her bending over a little
child in her lap, singing softly for
pure joy,—and the child was himself. There was a thought of her lifting a little child to the breast that had
borne him as a burden and a pain, to
nourish him there as a comfort and a
treasure,—and the child was himself.
There was a thought of her watching

and tending and guiding a little child
from day to day, from year to year,
putting tender arms around him,
bending over his first wavering steps,
rejoicing in his joys, wiping away the
tears from his eyes, as he had never
tried to wipe her tears away,—and
the child was himself. She had done
everything for the child's sake, but
what had the child done for her sake?
And the child was himself: that was
what he had come to,—after the
nightfire had burned out, after the
darkness had grown thin and melted
in the thoughts that pulsed through it
like rapid waves of light,—that was
what he had come to in the early
morning: himself, a child in his
mother's arms.

Then he arose and went out of
the grotto softly, making the three-

fold sign of reverence; and the eyes of Mary followed him with kind looks.

Joseph of Nazareth was still waiting outside the door.

"How was it that you did not see the angels?" he asked. "Were you not with the other shepherds?"

"No," answered Ammiel, "I was asleep. But I have seen the mother and the child. Blessed be the house that holds them."

"You are strangely clad for a shepherd," said Joseph. "Where do you come from?"

"From a far country," replied Ammiel; "from a country that you have never visited."

"Where are you going now?" asked Joseph.

"I am going home," answered Ammiel, "to my mother's and my father's house in Galilee."

"Go in peace, friend," said Joseph.

And the sad shepherd took up his battered staff, and went on his way rejoicing.